Once in a Red Moon

A Novella by

R. T. Budd

Author of *Knight's Blessing*
and
The Deepest Wounds of War

ISBN: 1-4802-3043-X
ISBN-13: 9781480230439

Dedication

To my wife of forty years, Sue, who reluctantly consented to listen to excerpts of this tale and then begged me to stop because it was too creepy; and my little brother, Wade, a retired police officer who gave me invaluable insight into the technical aspects of law enforcement and traffic codes. Finally, and most importantly, this story is dedicated to those who have perished needlessly at the hands of those who refuse to think before they drink. May the former find peace in the glory of heaven above, and may the latter burn in the fiery pits of hell for all eternity!

Revenge is a dish best served hot!
–R.T. Budd

Contents

PROLOGUE

Once in a Blue Moon

For those who are unaware, the third full moon in a single season—winter, spring, summer, or fall—that has four full moons, is known as a blue moon. More traditionally though, a blue moon is the second full moon in the same calendar month. Why it's called a blue moon is speculative at best; however, history does record the moon appearing to be blue for a period of time due to volumes of volcanic ash dumped into the sky from enormous eruptions of monumental proportions originating on small island masses found in the boundless waters of the Earth's great oceans. This ash purportedly ascended into the upper atmosphere, creating a bluish appearance during the lunar phases of the only natural satellite forever locked in the grasp of the Earth's powerful gravitation pull. Because these exclusive events rarely occur in nature, the freakish episodes gave rise to the phrase, "once in a blue moon."

In 1946, an article in the March issue of *Sky and Telescope* magazine erroneously reported a blue moon as being, "the second full moon in the same calendar month," and that fallacious definition grew into fact for newer generations of wide-eyed stargazers.

Reportedly, the English even gave names to all their full moons of the summer season: the first being a Hay Moon, the second being a Corn Moon, and the third being a Harvest Moon, for obvious agricultural reasons. But when a fourth full moon appeared during the season, the third moon became the Blue Moon so the farmers' other three moons could remain in proper spatial order to suit their agrarian purposes.

In truth, a blue moon occurs about seven times in a nineteen-year period, or about once every 2.7 years. But this tale is not about the science of the moon, the planets, or the stars in galaxies billions of light years away. No, dear reader, this account involves the sweet taste of revenge. Regardless of whose definition is right or wrong, the good folks of Jefferson County, Kansas, would never again use the term "blue moon" after witnessing the final full moon on the 31st day in the month of October, in the Year of our Lord, Nineteen-Hundred and Sixty.

Chapter 1
Skip George

The sun rose steadily over the cloudless, eastern–Kansas horizon, ushering in the dawn of a new day. It was going to be another scorcher for sure. The county was bone dry and could use the rain, but that was not happening anytime soon. The morning radio host of KJEF a one-man, two-bit, static, AM station broadcasting from dawn to dusk out of a dilapidated, former one-car service station on a nearly deserted highway to Valley Falls—hit the highlights of the local non-news. He then paused for a moment to acknowledge the upcoming prerecorded tape of the regional weather report. George Summers groaned as he sat at his unassuming breakfast table, cradling a hot cup of joe between his beefy hands and mulling over the real estate ads from the *Valley Falls Weekly Examiner.* He certainly did not need some overeducated meteorologist from Kansas City babbling on and on about this weather front or that weather front to clarify the obvious. Of course it was going to be a god-awful, sultry day; even those retards down at the home could figure that one out!

George, who preferred to be called by his nickname, "Skip," took a guarded slurp of coffee and glanced at his wristwatch—the expensive kind, a genuine Rolex. By all rights, he should have hit the road some thirty minutes ago, but it didn't matter if he was a little late for work. In fact, it did not matter if he was a *lot* late for work. No one at the agency would notice. After all, he married the boss's daughter, and rank has its privileges you know. George's boss owned a homegrown, small-time business with half a dozen employees, and no one dared call him out about his repeated tardiness. No, Crown Prince George was entirely above any scrutiny from the lowly commoners at the office as long as his father-in-law held the reins of the largest real estate business in Jefferson County firmly in hand. Largest real estate agency in the county—big deal—a county with a population of 11,522! Still, Big John Kingsley raked in more money than most in this part of Kansas.

George despised his job with the agency, but being the teacher's pet did have its advantages. He might be the most useless and unproductive employee in the office, but his coworkers would not utter a single disparaging word of reproach—not to his face anyway. Oh, they might belittle or demean him behind his back during a smoke break or lunchtime, but George didn't care what the others thought of him. No sirree, not one tiny bit. Screw those bitter bastards! *They* were not the ones who had the intestinal fortitude to undertake the thankless burden of taking the chief's one-and-only, grotesquely overweight, and unattractive-to-boot daughter off his hands, and walking her down the aisle of holy matrimony!

Christ, what a fat, homely-looking bitch she was! How anyone ever found a wedding gown to fit that slovenly sow-of-a-wife of his, was beyond any human comprehension. And did Big John, proud father of the blushing bride, really need to waste thousands of dollars in cold, hard cash furnishing the top table for the bridal party with fine Noritake bone china dinnerware, exquisite Oneida sterling silver flatware, and Waterford crystal glassware for the reception dinner? Hell, George could have used all that extra dough to pad his own wallet! It wasn't like he hadn't earned it, standing up there at the altar beside that huge heifer in full, public view for all to see! No, the wedding guests wouldn't come right out and say it, but George knew what they were whispering behind his back during the ceremony. Besides, the new Mrs. George Summers did not require any *fine* this or *elegant* that. She had all the subtle manners of a barnyard hog rooting through slop in a pig trough. Yeah, his coworkers at the office could whine all they wanted about his slothful work at Papa's real estate business, but George was paying a steep price for his "Get Out of Jail Free" cards. Talk about charity work!

And now a year after the nuptials, Big John was grumbling about a grandchild, for God's sake! George dared not tell him he had not slept with his new bride since their wedding night; he just wouldn't understand. How could any father face the truth that his precious, little princess could make a man physically ill with her monstrous bulk? It was all he could do to muster the strength not to puke all over the honeymoon suite that night! Poor Gertrude Summers believed all the gagging noises her new husband was uttering in the dark were simply passionate, guttural sounds emanating from her lover's dreamy mouth, bearing true testimony to her extraordinary sexual prowess.

Shortly after that nightmarish episode, George swore he would never go down that road again! When he began offering questionable excuses for separate sleeping arrangements, Gertrude grew suspicious of her husband's sexual orientation. But she concluded "don't ask, don't tell" was a far better policy than outright confrontation. As far as George was concerned, Big John could grouse all he wanted about grandchildren; there was absolutely no way he was ever mounting that beast of a wife again! He wasn't worried that Daddy's little angel would tattle on him or cause a big fuss. No, she would be too embarrassed to complain to father about her intimate sex life—or lack thereof. Gertrude had a wedding band on her finger, and that was good enough to suit her.

George "Skip" Summers peeked at his Rolex once again. *Hell,* he thought, *might as well get going before the old lady gets up.* George folded his paper in half, tossed it on the table, and then stood up while taking a final gulp of coffee. *Blah, enough of this shit. I need some hard stuff to get me going.* He poured the remaining brew in the kitchen sink, opened a nearby cupboard, and retrieved a bottle of Wild Cur—a local brand of illegally-distilled whiskey from neighboring Leavenworth County—which he had hidden way behind several boxes of king-size breakfast cereals. He took several swigs of the moonshine and wiped the dribble with his shirtsleeve. *Ah, now that's the good stuff,* he beamed with satisfaction.

Dearest Gertrude did not approve of her husband's alcohol dependence, and when an opportunity presented itself, she did not hesitate to pour the contents of the liquor bottles she chanced upon down the nearest drain. They argued about his drinking from time to time, but the heated discussions always ended the same way.

"I just don't understand why you have to drink so much," Gertrude would sob.

"Because I like it," he would reply.

"I think you're an alcoholic, George."

"Get off my back, Gertie! I can stop anytime I want to!"

"Then why don't you stop it right now?" she would blubber like a wounded child.

"I don't want to, that's why!" George would shout back at her.

"But if you really loved me..."

"Bingo!" he would scream, slapping his thigh.

It would take a moment for reality to set in, and then Gertrude would quickly shift emotional gears—launching into her faux offensive and threatening dire consequences for his insensitivity. "You'd better watch your step mister, or I just might find me another man!"

George, knowing full well it was all a ruse, would laugh out loud and wish her the best of luck. "You'd be doing the both of us a huge favor, Gertie dear."

Her false bravado then exposed, she'd suddenly burst into a torrent of crocodile tears and scamper off to the solace of her bedroom down the hall, shrieking all the while like a crazed baboon in heat.

Presently, George tucked the bottle of booze safely into his jacket pocket, snatched the car keys off the aqua-colored Formica countertop—he hated that shade of green, but it was Gertie's choice—and headed out the door. He hopped behind the wheel of his father-in-law's wedding gift: a 1959 El Dorado Seville. Yeah, the luxury Cadillac coupe with distinctive, huge, sharp tail fins and dual-bullet taillights. George keyed the ignition and cranked the 390-cubic-inch engine to life. Ah, the sweet sound of 345 horses all working together as one: music to the ears of any consummate connoisseur of fine automobiles. As George Summers swung his sedan north onto US Federal Route 59 toward Oskaloosa—steering wheel in one hand and a half-empty bottle of booze in the other—the man in the driver's seat had no inkling he would never make it to work on that sizzling summer's day.

Chapter 2
One Hundred Bottles of Beer on the Wall

The youngsters were excited. Eighteen young, energetic, nine- and ten-year-old, Little League ballplayers from the sticks were eager to board the big, yellow school bus and head toward Kansas City for the experience of a lifetime. Most of the boys had never seen a major-league baseball game before, which would be a special memory for any Little Leaguer in and of itself, but this day was even better. This was Monday, July 11, 1960, and baseball's annual Major League All-Star game would be played in Municipal Stadium, home of the Kansas City Athletics. It was the first of two All-Star games that year—the second to be played in New York City several weeks later. The big KC was all decked out to welcome baseball's best: Willie Mays, Hank Aaron, Roberto Clemente, Bill Mazeroski, Eddie Mathews, Mickey Mantle, Brooks Robinson, Yogi Berra, Ted Williams, Stan Musial, Bob Friend, Al Kaline, Orlando Cepeda, Luis Aparicio, and Ernie Banks, who happened to play with the Kansas City Monarchs of the Negro League before moving up to the "Bigs" with the Chicago Cubs. Sodas, hot dogs, peanuts, and Cracker Jacks; the Little Leaguers of Jefferson County truly did not care if they ever got back. Oh, what a glorious day it would be! Eighteen little men full of piss and vinegar, two adult chaperones ready to pull out their hair, and one prehistoric bus driver. He had a pair of plastic, black-rimmed, prescription glasses—held together with white adhesive tape—and a shiny, gold-capped tooth.

After a quick count of the kids and corresponding check marks on the clipboard, finally, all were present and accounted for. It was time to get the show on the road! The folding-glass door on the school bus opened wide, and the adults desperately tried to control the frenzied throng. It was no use. The wide-eyed, fanatical kids were boarding the vehicle on their own terms. Not even John Wayne and a gang of his *Red River* cattle drovers could halt this stampede! But who could blame them? This was a day they would remember all their lives. In less than a minute's time, the eager beavers stormed aboard the yellow coach and settled into their seats.

"ALL RIGHT, GENTLEMEN!" boomed an authoritative voice over the youthful commotion in the bus. "Let's settle down so I can get one final head count."

Coach Nixon began his tally. He was interrupted several times by the boisterous youngsters, causing him to start his roll call over from the very beginning. Meanwhile, the natives grew restless.

"Come on, Coach," one of the boys whined. "We're going to be late for the game, for crying out loud."

"Just hold your horses, sonny boy. Game time is one o'clock. We've got plenty of time to get to the zoo and the ballpark," the coach reassured his young charge.

"Do we really have to go to the zoo, Coach?" another boy moaned.

"Yeah, Coach, we'd rather get to the stadium early and watch warm-ups and batting practice," a third youngster chimed in.

Coach Nixon didn't feel the need to tell his kids the truth of the matter; after all, they really didn't need to know. The boys worked their little hearts out selling subs door-to-door, washing cars, peddling magazine subscriptions, and a host of other fund-raising activities to accumulate enough money to get to Kansas City's Municipal Stadium for the ball game. It wasn't their fault they fell far short of their financial goal. It wasn't their fault all their quarters, nickels, and dimes didn't come near to covering the expenses involved for such an excursion. As the old cliché goes, it's always darkest before the dawn.

Coach Nixon, who worked as a sales assistant at the local hardware store, had a lovely wife named Monica. Mrs. Nixon, the former Monica Sue Bower, was an elementary school teacher, and her older brother, Gerald Bower, was a high school chemistry teacher. Gerald also chaired the finance committee for the Jefferson County Board of Education. It was Gerald—an avid baseball fan and the father of a ten-year-old who played shortstop for the Little Buffs—who devised an ingenious scheme to convert the Little Leaguers' baseball outing into a legitimate, school field trip to visit the Kansas City Zoo; an academic activity that technically, if not ethically, qualified for Jefferson County School District funding. After all, Gerald reasoned, wouldn't it be a shame to travel all the way to Kansas City and back just to see some boring, domesticated, "wild" animals tucked away in tiny cages? The Kansas City ballpark was only a stone's throw away.

As Gerald figured it, the only possible bump in the road would be certifying the trip as a "learning" experience. He hurdled that obstacle with ease by making a quick call to the zoo administration office in Kansas City. The friendly administrative assistant on the other end of the line assured him that Missouri and Kansas state standards offered academic credits in sciences, social studies, and communication arts for a program at the zoo entitled, "Journey to Survival." The forty-five–minute presentation was designed to help school students discover various reasons for animal endangerment around the world. That sealed the deal. Not only was the outing given the school board's wholehearted blessing and financial support, they also suggested using a district school bus for transportation to and from the event at the taxpayers' expense.

All that remained was procuring tickets for a Kansas City Athletics' ball game. Normally seating at that venue was pricy at best, but Gerald had an old college chum from his undergraduate days at Kansas State University who now worked in the front office for the Kansas City Athletics. So Gerald made a phone call.

"Jerry, how are you doing, old buddy?" came a voice over the telephone line.

"Great, Clark. How about you?" Gerald asked out of courtesy.

"Fine, fine. Long time, no hear from you, Jerry boy. What've you been up to?"

"Not much," Gerald replied. "Still trying to teach these Kansas country kids some high school chemistry, you know."

"How's the wife and kids, Jer?"

"Just fine. Jerry Junior is ten, and Marissa is six. She starts first grade this fall."

"Wow—ten and six! Jesus, they do grow up quick, don't they?" Clark said.

"They sure do. Blink an eye, and they're off to college before you know it. How about you, Clark? Meet Mrs. Right yet?"

"Heck, no; I'm too busy doing the bachelor thing. Besides, you know what a slob I am. I mean, we were roommates at State for four years. You seriously think the woman's been born yet that could put up with that?"

Gerald laughed. "No, Clark, I guess not."

"So what's on your mind, Jerry? It's not like a get a phone call from you every day, you know?"

"Well first of all, I'd like to remind you of that jam I got you out of during our junior year at State. Remember?"

"Uh oh, Jerry. This sounds like blackmail to me," Clark said with humor in his voice.

"No, no," Gerald chuckled. "It's nothing like that, Clark. I just wanted to refresh your memory a bit before I asked you for a favor."

"Shoot."

"Well, me being a fine, upstanding citizen in the local community and all, I got myself roped into the local county Little League program this year. These are some really good kids, Clark. We're even sending one of our teams to regionals this year, and who knows? We might even make it to states."

"That's great, Jer. Congratulations! So what can I do for you, Mr. Commissioner?"

"Well, these kids have really worked hard this year, and most of them have never seen a big-league baseball game before..."

"Say no more, buddy. Just tell me what game you'd like to see, and how many tickets you'll need. Of course, keep in mind the stadium only holds about 30,000 fans, and the best I can do is a 10-percent discount."

"Gee, Clark that would be great! Some game in July would fit nicely into our summer schedule. We would have eighteen boys, the coach, me, and one bus driver in the group. Think you could swing that?"

"No problem. You say most of these kids have never been to a professional ballgame before?" Clark asked.

"That's right, Clark. I know we're not that far away from Kansas City, but most folks in Jefferson County are just ordinary farmers scratching out a living from day to day. They don't have the time or money for recreational getaways, but they do love their baseball around these parts."

"Well then, Jer, why don't we make this something really special to remember?" Clark suggested.

"What do you mean?"

"Well, let's not waste time on some ordinary, everyday baseball game..."

Gerald could not believe his ears when he heard his old college mate offer lower box-seat tickets for $7.50 apiece to the upcoming All-Star game at Kansas City's Municipal Stadium! That would certainly give the kids the treat they deserved, and at cut-rate prices to boot.

Although Gerald Bower had hit the ball out of the park as far as saving money for the Kansas City excursion, there were plenty of other financial burdens to consider. Traditional, run-of-the-mill fund-raisers wouldn't begin to fill the till for future endeavors. A trip to regionals would not be cheap; and if they made it to the state tournament, well that was certainly a horse of a different color. The folks around Jefferson County didn't have a lot of extra dough socked away in their cookie jars for charitable donations to a Little League baseball team. And what about the Little League World Series in Williamsport, Pennsylvania—wouldn't that be something? True, their chances were slim; but this year's crop of Little Leaguers was the best that anyone could remember in these parts. The Little Buffs were 22-0 at this point, and that included creaming some highbrow teams from the surrounding larger towns and big cities. Sure, Williamsport might only be a pipe dream; but to these kids, nothing was impossible. Gerald was determined not to let them down. He needed to play every angle and cut every corner he could to ensure his boys needn't be concerned about the financial aspects of their season. Although the Little Leaguers from Jefferson County might not like it—nor would they ever discover the rationale for putting the Kansas City Zoo on their baseball agenda—they would have to just buck up and do it anyway.

Coach Nixon placed a final check mark on his clipboard roster, and seemed satisfied with the total. "Okay boys, settle down and listen up!" the coach ordered. "Everybody got their baseball mitts?" The kids gladly waved their gloves high in the air. "Jerry, you've got the tickets, right?"

"Don't worry, Coach," Gerald patted his knapsack on the seat beside him. "I've got everything right here."

"Sam..." the coach said, nodding at the driver.

"Yes, sir?" the old man responded.

"Let's get rolling."

"Yes, sir!" the senior chauffeur beamed, his single gold tooth gleaming in the early morning sunlight.

The big, yellow school bus stubbornly ground into first gear, then into second as the vehicle exited the parking lot, turning south onto US Federal Route 59. As the bus picked up speed, one of the older boys started a chorus of "One Hundred Bottles of Beer on the Wall." Coach Nixon only hoped the bus was out of earshot of the proud parents in the parking lot, who were still waving good-byes to their innocent, little progenies.

Chapter 3
DUI

George "Skip" Summers was more than just a little buzzed as he roared down the two-lane highway behind the wheel of his pricy Cadillac Coupe. Yeah, he'd heard all the public safety propaganda urging motorists not to drink and drive—so what? That mindless mumbo jumbo might apply to all those other scatterbrains out there who couldn't hold their liquor, but it certainly didn't apply to him. No sir. Skip could drink anyone under the table and still have all his wits about him!

That's what he believed anyway, as he took another swig from his half-empty bottle of whiskey, unknowingly veering from one side of the road to the other. His friends—including his family physician—tried to warn him about the inherent dangers of excessive drinking, but what did they know? Hell, if they were tied down to a hideous, behemoth of a wife, and trapped in a wretched, humdrum job in a tiny office with absolutely no tangible responsibilities, they just might stare at the empty bottoms of a few bottles of booze as well! Just like the old adage goes: before you criticize me, try walking a mile in my shoes. What did other people know about how he had to look into the mirror every day, confronting the materialistic man standing before him—a shell of a human being who sold his self-respect and very soul to the devil himself in exchange for a few trinkets? If only he could rewind the tape of his life, he would do things differently. Or would he?

The custom, tail-finned Caddy continued rocketing down Route 59 without any regard to the posted speed limit. Skip wasn't worried about some cop pulling him over for speeding. His father-in-law was an associate member of the Fraternal Order of Police, and buddy-buddy with every law-enforcement officer in Jefferson County—all two of them. Skip had been stopped for a variety of traffic violations on numerous occasions in the past, and never received as much as a warning for his negligence behind the wheel. Of course, it didn't hurt that the sheriff of Jefferson County and his deputy were the younger brothers of his father-in-law, Big John Kingsley! The Kansas Highway Patrol was not known to routinely work this section of Route 59, but Skip was almost certain Big Daddy Kingsley probably had a few of those lawmen in his back pocket as well.

Little Brenda Lee's big voice boomed out "I'm Sorry," her latest in a string of hits playing over the El Dorado's premium sound system, as the gleaming Cadillac roared down the asphalt motorway. Waves of summer heat vacillated upward from the sunbaked pavement. It was only 8:30 in the morning, but the mercury in the thermometer was already climbing toward the 90-degree mark. *God,* Skip thought to himself as he downed another swig of whiskey from his near-empty bottle, *how could it possibly get any hotter today?*

Skip wiped a dribble of alcohol from his unshaven chin and refocused his attention—which was foggy, at best—to the road up ahead. "What the hell is that?" he mumbled out loud. Identifying something through his huge windshield in the blistering heat of the day was like trying to make out a vague mirage in the distant desert. "Is that a dog?" Skip said, talking to himself again. "Hell, yes." He squinted through murky eyes, "That is a dog!" Skip tightened his grip on the steering wheel and gritted his teeth. "Who in the hell does he think he is, standing in the middle of the highway like that? Does he think he owns this road? Mangy mutt! I'll teach him a lesson, by God!"

There was no excuse for what Skip was contemplating in his pickled head. He had plenty of room to drive past the wayward canine on his side of the two-lane, country road; but he was dead set on running the stray hound straight into the ground without any quarter given. He didn't care if it caused damage to his sedan; the insurance company would take care of that. Even if they didn't, his father-in-law would. Besides, how much damage could a dog actually do to his two-ton, iron horse?

Skip sucked down the last of his booze and tossed the empty bottle over toward the passenger's seat. He mashed the gas pedal to the floor, picked up speed, and zoomed toward his unsuspecting victim, bearing down on his target using the imaginary crosshairs in his mind's eye. At the very last second, Skip crossed over the solid, double, yellow line dividing Route 59 into right and left lanes.

KA-THUD! The poor, dumb animal never knew what hit him. As the maniacal driver screamed out a rebel yell, the black Lab–Setter mix was launched across the roadway. He came to rest in a drainage ditch some thirty yards away, all 320 bones in his body crushed beyond recognition. Reveling in his own wretched act of violence, Skip was too far past the point of sobriety to clearly appreciate the large vehicle cresting the hill just in front of him. He did notice a flashing, yellow blur, and heard the blaring horn warning of impending disaster—but it was too late for Skip to navigate his massive automobile back into his own lane to avoid a serious collision.

Fortunately for Skip, the impact of the two motor vehicles was not directly head-on. Unfortunately for the bus, the sideswipe caused it to skid off the road, crash through the guardrail, and tumble down a thirty-foot embankment near a heavily wooded area. With metal parts crunching, safety glass shattering, and frantic passengers screaming all the while, the crumpled school bus finally came to rest on its flattened rooftop. For a moment, there was an eerie silence from the bottom of the hill, like the misleading calm before an impending storm.

Meanwhile, Skip managed to brake his classy Caddy to a stop on the shoulder of Route 59, several hundred feet down the road from the accident site. He wasn't quite sure what had just transpired, but he knew it wasn't good, and he knew it wasn't a dream. He slowly opened the hefty door of his El Dorado, and extracted himself from the driver's seat. It took a moment for Skip to get his bearings as he turned one way, and then another. Finally he looked back down the highway, shielding his bloodshot eyes from the glaring, morning sun. Some distance down the road, he thought he saw a set of black tire marks tracking down the pavement, veering to the right, and then disappearing altogether over the shoulder of the deserted highway. It was extraordinarily quiet—almost too quiet. Maybe it was a dream after all.

"I'm sorry, so sorry," Brenda Lee crooned over the car radio, bringing Skip back down to planet Earth. As reality set in, Skip's conscious brain commanded him to race back toward the accident scene to see what could be done to assist the poor victims in the other vehicle. Skip wanted to run, but his whole body shivered. His legs were so weak, he found it difficult to walk—much less run—back down the road. Was he in shock or was it the effects of the booze? In truth, it was probably a little of both. Ultimately, he willed what inner strength he could muster and stumbled forward, hoping some Good Samaritan would soon pass by and stop to render aid. *Wait a minute,* Skip suddenly speculated. *What the devil am I thinking? If anyone sees this catastrophe, they'll figure out what I've done for sure. They'll know that I'm responsible for this mess!* But what the "mess" was, was not entirely clear yet.

Skip picked up his forward momentum, now anxious to uncover the full scope of his present predicament before someone else did. As he neared the final segment of freshly-made skid marks now indelibly etched into the weather-worn pavement beneath his feet, he encountered the overpowering odor of burnt rubber. It permeated every nook and cranny of his throbbing nostrils.

Skip thought he heard a faint, creaky noise reverberating from somewhere just over the berm's edge. It was a strange sort of cyclical sound, punctuated by several seconds of silence. It sounded like a rusty hinge on a garden gate moving to and fro in the wind of a gusty day, desperately crying out for a soothing spot of relief from the kindhearted Tin Man's oilcan.

Squeak, squeak, squeak ... squeak, squeak, squeak ... squeak, squeak, squeak...

Skip didn't want to peep over the earthen bank, but ultimately curiosity got the better of him. He cautiously navigated his way through the shattered pieces of wooden guardrail, and glanced over the steep embankment.

The rumpled mass of metal and broken glass that once resembled an untarnished school bus now lay helplessly stagnant on its damaged, yellow roof. One of its front wheels, slightly askew, crazily wobbled about on its mutilated axel.

Squeak, squeak, squeak ... squeak, squeak, squeak ... squeak, squeak, squeak...

Other than that one, solitary sound, there was absolutely nothing else stirring under the searing heat of the morning sun. Not a bird, not a mouse, not a leaf in the trees, not a vehicle from the highway above—nothing. Absolutely nothing at all. Curiously, the upended school bus reminded Skip of a slowly-dying cockroach lying helplessly on its back.

As far as Skip could tell from his vantage point, no one was moving from within the crippled bus below. He wiped the dripping beads of alcohol-saturated perspiration from his furrowed brow, racking his aching brain to make some sense out of a senseless situation.

What happened just a few minutes ago? The dog... That damn dog! If it wasn't for that mangy mongrel!

But Skip wasn't *that* drunk. He knew it wouldn't take accident investigators long to blow a hole in that flimsy explanation.

"So, Mr. Summers, is it?" an Inspector Colombo impersonator would drone in his gravelly, monotone voice while sporting an ancient, faded trench coat and munching on the stubble of a stale, smokeless, Dutch

Masters stogie. "*It seems the canine in question was plastered smack-dab in the middle of the eastbound lane while you, sir, were traveling westbound on Route 59 on your way to work. Does that about sum it up, sir?*" The interrogation would then continue after a brief pause and an affirmative nod from the prime suspect. "*My only question left for you then, sir, is what in the devil were you doing driving your vehicle over in the eastbound lane?*" Case closed!

And what about the inevitable field-sobriety test and follow-up blood-alcohol draws in the emergency room at Jefferson County Community Hospital? Then his goose would be cooked for sure! On the other hand, if he fled the scene of the accident, it would not take long for the authorities to track him down, chuck him in the slammer, and throw away the keys! *What in God's name am I to do?* Skip wondered desperately.

Summers knew the incessant heat and quart of whiskey surging throughout his body were clouding his better judgment, but he had to make a decision soon. Be it right, wrong, or indifferent, any decision was better than none at all. And then he heard it. Something or someone down there was calling out for help! It was a feeble attempt at best, but Skip could hear it nonetheless. He took a step closer to the edge of the overhang. Yes, there it was again. Someone needed help—perhaps the driver. Maybe there was only one person in the vehicle. Maybe one guy was all there was, driving a school bus from point A to point B with no passengers aboard. The possibility of a single, nonfatal injury gave Skip pause for relief.

A moment later, his hopes were forever dashed as a heart-wrenching chorus of ghastly groans drifted upward from the wreckage below. Even in his impaired condition, Skip knew there was more than just a single bus driver in that carnage: some of the victims were probably seriously injured, and some might possibly be deader than dead!

It was decision time. He had to do something. He had to commit himself one way or the other. He was either going to stay and do what he could to help those poor souls down there, or he was going to get the hell out of Dodge City as quickly as he was able. It was now or never, do or die!

As fate would have it, Skip didn't have to make up his mind one way or the other; he didn't have to do anything at all. As the smell of gasoline fumes filled his nostrils, a small plume of smoke rose from the broken rubble at the base of the hill. An instant later the bus burst into blistering flames, sending a brilliant fireball soaring high into the cloudless, morning sky. It knocked Skip flat on his back. A moment later, everything went black.

He didn't know how long he had lain there alongside the shoulder of Route 59. He didn't know if he had passed out or was knocked unconscious by the terrible explosion at the bottom of the ravine. His head was still groggy, but he did sense there was someone with him now—someone offering a few comforting words.

"Skip, are you all right?" a familiar voice asked.

Slowly, Skip opened his eyes and focused on the face looking down at him. Instantly, he felt his heart skip a beat; it was a uniformed police officer of some sort.

"Skip," the lawman softly said. "Can you hear me, son?"

"Yeah," Skip managed, shielding his eyes from the bright sunlight overhead. He tried to zero in on the face that was speaking to him.

"Skip," the man comforted. "It's me, Mark Kingsley."

Skip heaved a sigh of relief as he finally matched the face with the voice. It was Deputy Sheriff Mark Kingsley, one of his wife's three older uncles. "Don't you worry, boy. We're going to get you out of this mess."

Later that evening, the biggest, brightest full moon the residents of Jefferson County had ever witnessed climbed high into the sky through the balmy Kansas air. The mythical man whose face was etched upon the crater-pocked surface of the lunar orb appeared noticeably somber as he looked down upon the Earth below. He would not smile again until just before the Thanksgiving holiday season of November 1960, some four months hence.

Chapter 4
The Kingsley Clan

The entire accident investigation was a farce. Skip never underwent a field-sobriety check or submitted to a test for blood-alcohol levels. After a "comprehensive" examination of Sam Hetrick's remains, the county coroner concluded the elderly driver must have suffered a fatal heart attack behind the wheel, causing him to lose control of the school bus. Although the longtime district employee had no medical history of a heart condition, and his body was almost incinerated in the fiery blast, somehow the medical examiner found sufficient evidence to officially list the cause of death as "cardiac arrest."

That being done, the county sheriff and his lone deputy had little difficulty reconstructing the incident. Sam Hetrick had an acute coronary, veered into oncoming traffic, sideswiped Skip's El Dorado, then crossed back over the double yellow line, through the guardrail, and into the ravine. KABOOM! It was an open-and-shut case. Twenty-one fatalities; the worst vehicular accident in the United States since the school-bus tragedy in California two years earlier that claimed the lives of twenty-six school children and the driver. The Jefferson County accident made the front page of the local newspapers, was relegated to page three in the national broadsheets, and given thirty seconds on the evening news of the three major TV networks. After all, it was a presidential election year—a projected contest between Richard M. Nixon and John F. Kennedy—and twenty-one lives snuffed out in a traffic accident in rural Kansas were essentially inconsequential in the grander scheme of things. Had the real story leaked out, scores of newshounds would have descended upon Jefferson County in an instant. Skip, scrutinized beneath the media microscopes, would have provided several extra months of sordid entertainment. But the truth would never be known by anyone apart from Skip and the four co-conspirators: Big John Kingsley, Sheriff Matt Kingsley, Deputy Sheriff Mark Kingsley, and County Coroner Luke Kingsley. All were sworn to carry the despicable details of the accident to their graves. Yes, the Kingsley clan would make everything right for Skip and sweet, little Gertie—whatever the cost.

Chapter 5
Rest in Peace

Like most populated areas of the Midwest, Jefferson County had its share of cemeteries scattered here and there, but only one funeral home. It was located in Oskaloosa, the county seat. In fact, most of the local residents joked on occasion that since the first Europeans settled in eastern Kansas in the 1830s, there were probably ten-fold more dead in Jefferson County than living. Even with outside help, it would have taken months to sort the remains and positively identify all the charred corpses from the terrible bus crash. The bodies were wholly grotesque. They looked as though they might have been Oscar Mayer wieners carelessly dropped from an improvised skewer into a roaring campfire: surreally shriveled into scorched, black masses and helplessly lying upon a beach of red-hot coals.

With the aid of dental records, the three adults were the only members of the fatal outing identified with any reasonable certainty—and even then, it was no easy task. As the unwitting scapegoat of the terrible tragedy—and with no witnesses to defend him—Sam Hetrick's funeral service went virtually unattended. The Kingsley-clan cover-up left the local community believing Hetrick was the lone culprit of the whole dreadful affair.

It was initially conjectured several of the boys might be identified by religious medallions worn around their necks, or possibly the watches strapped about their wrists. It soon became evident that the intense heat generated by the bus explosion practically vaporized any personal items the boys may have been wearing on that awful, fateful day. Dental records were of no use because the kids of rural Jefferson County did not make routine visits to the local dentist. After lengthy delays and little progress, the parents of the boys unanimously decided to lay their children down together in a common grave located in the geographical center of the county. It was a solemn ceremony, attended by hundreds and hundreds of disconsolate mourners and well-wishers from all around the Sunflower State. For the first week or so after the funeral service, inquisitive visitors continued to patronize the gravesite, laying wreaths or lighting candles in remembrance. Eventually interest waned, and soon the eighteen youngsters—each lying beneath the newly quarried ground in their small, nondescript, white, wooden caskets—ceased to exist in the minds of the living. But there were certain persons who would never forget the tragedy: the families of the fallen, and more importantly, the boys themselves.

Chapter 6
Wasteland

The strange goings-on began, according to the locals, during the first new moon not long after the school-bus accident. It was a tiny plot of land—no more than an eighth of an acre in scope—with wooden posts and rails skirting the perimeter of the yard. An ordinary, single obelisk of polished granite stood at the epicenter of the memorial garden, bearing the engraved names of the misfortunate boys residing within the grounds and three, simple words, "Gone Too Soon."

An older, Negro gentleman, by the name of Quentin Jones believed it was his Christian duty to appoint himself as the charitable caretaker of the final resting place for the eighteen young boys. He attended the youngsters' graveside service weeks earlier, but out of respect for the grieving parents kept his distance on that solemn occasion. When the idea of becoming the custodian came to mind, Quentin didn't seek anyone's permission to tend the memorial plot, he just started doing it. It was simply God's will, and no one objected to the elderly man's spiritual calling.

No one in Jefferson County seemed to know much about Quentin's past. They didn't know where he came from, or how he ended up in that part of Kansas. He apparently appeared out of thin air some eighteen years earlier and was hired as a janitor for the Winchester elementary school. It was the same school the boys attended before their untimely deaths.

Some county residents speculated Quentin was a military veteran possibly discharged from nearby Fort Leavenworth during the World War II era. They conjectured he headed west from the army base after his release and ended his journey some twenty-five miles later in Jefferson County.

There were other citizens, however, who believed Quentin may have come from Fort Leavenworth all right, but it may have been through the iron gates of the United States Disciplinary Barracks located on the post. The USDB was the military's only maximum-security facility, housing male service members convicted at court-martial for violations of the

Uniform Code of Military Justice. Only enlisted members with sentences over five years, commissioned officers, and those prisoners convicted of offenses relating to national security were confined to the USDB.

Although many rumors circulated around the county, no one questioned Quentin about his past, and he did not volunteer any information in return. He was quiet, courteous, and performed his custodial duties at the school as well as anyone ever could. It wasn't long before Quentin gained the trust and respect of the good folks in the county.

Now recently retired after a number of years with the school district, the gentle janitor found himself with too much free time and in want of a useful hobby. Quentin never fancied himself a professional greenskeeper, but never for a moment did he believe he would have any difficulty establishing a suitable blanket of grass to shelter the remains of the ill-fated decedents resting below. He seeded, watered, fertilized, and faithfully tended his labor of love on a daily basis. Yet he could not get anything to sprout within the confines of the tiny cemetery—not even as much as an ordinary weed. No matter what the Good Samaritan tried or how long he toiled, the sacred plot refused to cooperate, remaining absolutely barren of all vegetation. "Ashes to ashes, and dust to dust…" and that was exactly what the 5,445-square-foot cemetery was—the ashes of the boys, and the dust of the bone-dry, unfertile ground.

Quentin began to think it odd when he redoubled his efforts to cultivate a lush carpet of green at the gravesite, and met with the same futile results he encountered when the youngsters were first laid to rest there some weeks past. How could it possibly be that just inside the wooden fence surrounding the hallowed ground lay a desolate section of mother earth, best described as layers of dust heaped upon layers of dust; yet on the far side of the railed boundary, a grand variety of indigenous grasses, flowers, and trees as lush as an oasis in the desert flourished in all their natural glory with no tending whatsoever? True, it had been a hot summer. But shortly after the boys' deaths the region was blessed with a generous amount of rainfall, keeping the Kansas countryside green and sparing it from drought. Those few passersby who ventured within eyesight of the graveyard found it a most peculiar scene, and could not begin to make heads or tails out of the mysterious landscape. The small parcel of wasteland was a very strange sight indeed!

Chapter 7
Denial

Skip Summers and wife, Gertrude, attended the funeral service for the deceased boys against the advice of Big John Kingsley himself. John and his three brothers were fearful Skip might have a mental meltdown during the memorial observance for the dearly departed and confess his reprehensible crime on the spot, implicating the entire Kingsley clan in the process.

But Skip remained indifferent to the whole affair. He was not apologetic, remorseful, or penitent. Why should he be? It wasn't his fault a group of rug rats on their way to a baseball game ended up in the wrong place at the wrong time. Skip even convinced himself it was the bus driver's fault for being an incompetent nincompoop! Why did the old fart have to lose control of the bus after sideswiping his Caddy? Did he really have to crash through the guardrail and plummet into the ravine?

Astonishingly, Skip somehow lost his grip on reality; brushing off the fact that *he* was the one in the wrong lane. *He* was the one who was plastered and driving under the influence. *He* was the one who slammed into a dumb animal for sport. *He* was the one who caused the fatal crash that took twenty-one innocent lives. By this point, Skip lost complete touch with any semblance of sanity concerning the catastrophic event. He even entertained the idea of contacting an attorney to pursue the possibility of suing the county school board for employing an inept bus driver! When Big John learned of his son-in-law's outrageous scheme, he paid Skip an impromptu visit and read him the riot act.

"You'd better get your act together, son, and pray to God no one ever learns the truth about what really happened! The sooner this boatload of shit that you're spreading around blows over, the better. Is that clear?" Big John yelled.

"Yeah, whatever," Skip glared.

"And one more thing," Big John demanded.

"What's that?" Skip inquired disingenuously.

"You'd better put some *extra* effort into getting me my grandson, Skip. You catch my drift?"

Skip caught his drift all right, but there was no way in hell he was climbing back into bed with that pig of a daughter of his! Skip was smart enough not to come right out and tell Big John that, though. He would let the sleeping dog lie. Skip would let the sleeping pig lie as well!

Chapter 8
Nightmare

He could smell the horrendous stench of burning human flesh swirling through every nook and cranny of his nasal cavity. He could taste the charred body parts piercing the tiny buds on the coarse surface of his tainted tongue. He could see with his mind's eye the terrified boys on the stricken bus clawing at the windows, struggling to escape the horrific flames creeping up from behind. Try as they might, they could not break free from the advancing inferno as the thick, black smoke blinded their vision and choked off the oxygen supply they so desperately needed for their little lungs to survive. He heard them scream out for mercy, pleading for someone to pluck them from the strengthening blaze. But God was not listening to their prayers of deliverance; Skip just stood there at the summit, frozen in suspended animation. He was paralyzed with indifference as the fire consumed the Little Leaguers one by one, melting their small, shrieking faces like hot wax liquescing on a candlestick. He wanted to look away but could not. It was as though his head was gripped in an invisible vice forcing him to stare directly at the dreadful carnage. He was powerless to close his eyes to the evolving mayhem. The more he struggled to flee the tragedy, the heavier his earthly legs grew. It felt as though the ground beneath his feet suddenly softened, transforming the heretofore-solid terrain into a pit of treacherous quicksand. His helpless body descended deeper and deeper into an unfathomable quarry of no return.

Skip woke up screaming and thrashing wildly about. His pajamas were soaking wet, and the bed linens were drenched in perspiration that smelled of liquor. It took him several moments to reorient himself to time and space in the darkness lurking there in his bedroom. Still visibly shaken, and chilled to the marrow from his frightening nightmare, he reached out toward the bedside stand and snatched the metal alarm clock from its perch with a trembling hand. The luminescent dial on the circular timepiece read a quarter past four.

Damn, he cursed his aching head. *When will I be able to sleep straight through the night again?*

Skip's friends—those casual acquaintances who were loyal buddies as long as he was buying rounds down at the bar—assured him he would get back to normal in due time. Due time? What the hell was due time? How long was due time? Although the local amateur shrinks couldn't offer Skip an exact date, they did manage to offer him free bits of advice. "You know, Skip, it's not unusual for those involved in an accident such as yours to naturally feel some sense of guilt and responsibility for the mishap—even though you had absolutely no real part in the result of the tragedy itself. In time, you will come to terms with that reality, and finally be at peace with yourself."

No real part in the crash? Not my fault? Ha! If the unwitting fellows only knew the truth, the whole truth, and nothing but the truth, they'd sure whistle a different tune, then, by God! Skip held his pounding skull between his cold, clammy hands and pressed inward as hard as he could. Maybe, just maybe he had a conscience after all. Maybe there were a few fragments of morality still smoldering deep inside his pickled brain. The brooding man sat up and swung his legs over the bedside. *A little after four in the wee hours of the morning,* he thought to himself dejectedly. *Damn it to hell!* He tossed the alarm clock back on the nightstand, flicked on the table lamp, and reached out for his trusty, old companion sitting nearby. Skip twisted the cap off his bottle of Wild Cur and took several long, deep swallows of the demon whiskey. Although the effects were only temporary, it would get him through the rest of the night. He turned off the light and repositioned himself in the twin bed once again, cradling the bottle of booze in his arms like a child with his favorite teddy bear. Moments later Skip was sound asleep, snoring to beat the band.

Chapter 9
Fog

It was the dead of night: the time when spectral spirits arise from their earthly tombs to plague the mortal world with deeds of dark revenge. The first sliver of soft, lunar light appeared from above as the new moon cordially acquiesced to its timeless successor in imperceptible but measured increments. Not long after, a thick band of miasma descended upon the place that had become known as the Eighth Acre. Unlike the city of London in faraway England, Jefferson County, Kansas, was not renowned for its foggy weather. In fact, a great number of its 11,522 residents—give or take a few—had never experienced the meteorological condition categorized as "fog." Yet there it was, hovering above the hallowed field of the Eighth Acre. And beneath that milky, clouded veil of vapor, unusual events began to unfold.

Chapter 10
Six Names

Quentin Jones reported for duty as he regularly did every day of every week since the melancholy, graveside service. It was the second week of August, and the victims of the terrible accident were barely four-weeks deceased. In spite of the ceaseless efforts of caretaker Jones to transform the desolate spot into a garden of serenity, not a single seed of any sort had blossomed into a solitary blade of grass within the confines of the Eighth Acre.

Although the plot lay as barren as ever, there was still something different on this early Tuesday morning that eluded Mr. Jones at first glance. It wasn't until he reached the center of the garden that he noticed the first sign of intrusion near the site of its memorial granite stone. Directly beneath the caption, "Gone Too Soon," was an alphabetical listing of the dearly departed in three columns, with six names in each column.

"What the devil…" Quentin mumbled to himself as he eyed the commemorative monument at arm's length with no one else around to hear.

What caught the self-appointed, elderly custodian's attention was this: only yesterday morning, all eighteen names inscribed on the slab were clearly visible; yet this morning, only twelve remained! Quentin paused a moment to remove his spectacles from his face. He snatched a red bandana from his left breast pocket and thoroughly scrubbed his glasses before putting them on again. Perhaps the monument had sunk a foot or so into the ground under its own massive weight, was Quentin's first rational thought. But under closer scrutiny, the man of senior years ultimately concluded that was not the case at all. No, the stone itself had not moved an inch. Instead, the bottom two lines originally inscribed on the face of the granite obelisk—a total of six names all together—had simply disappeared into thin air!

Chapter 11
Earl Scrap's Scrap Yard

It was near dusk when Mark Kingsley's patrol car passed the auto salvage yard belonging to Earl Scrap. The deputy sheriff was on routine patrol cruising down Route 59 on a lazy, summer evening. The shift thus far was uneventful, as it usually was, and the officer was seriously considering pulling off onto a side road for some snooze time. He was supposed to stop at Earl's place and check the padlock on the security fence, but he rarely did. After all, it was only a graveyard for old clunkers and bashed-up vehicles that were far past their prime. It wasn't like someone was going to break in and drive away with some fancy, luxury automobile worth $10,000. Even if a would-be thief managed to penetrate the twelve-foot-high security fence ringing the perimeter of the business, there was still one more obstacle the unwitting robber would face—a Rottweiler/Pit-bull mix by the name of Genghis Khan. By all accounts, he was the most ferocious canine in the tri-county area. Anyone who knew anything about Earl's place knew about Khan, and knew to steer clear of the place after hours. A customer once asked Earl, out of simple curiosity, what kind of dog food Khan liked to eat. Earl scratched his head and then told the man he didn't feed the mongrel anything special; he'd just toss his pooch an old, rusty bumper from a wreck in his scrap yard every now and then.

As Deputy Sheriff Kingsley approached Earl Scrap's Scrap Yard, he slowed his squad car down to get a quick eyeball on the place, never intending to stop. Suddenly he thought he saw something moving near the rear of the yard through the waning light of the early-evening sunset. It may have only been old Khan on the prowl, but Kingsley was almost certain whatever he saw out of the corner of his eye was probably not a dog. He decided he'd better check it out.

After making a U-turn in the middle of the highway, he drove back down the road a short distance, navigated his vehicle into the gravel parking area near the front gate, and came to a stop. From his vantage point in the squad car, the padlocked chain on the gate seemed to be secure. Maybe he was just seeing things. He hadn't had a cup of coffee for several hours now; maybe he needed a shot of caffeine to perk him up. Kingsley was about to dismiss the whole matter when a peculiar thought crossed his mind. *Where was Khan, the junkyard dog?* Normally the frenzied beast would be leaping around at the entrance, barking and howling up a storm. God help the person within a mile of Earl's place if the crazy canine crashed through the security fence and had you in his sights!

Kingsley decided it was much too quiet at the junkyard for the place to be normal. He climbed out of his cruiser, put on his uniform cap, adjusted his utility belt, and habitually felt for his service revolver just to be sure it was where it should be. At the last second, he decided to retrieve his twelve-gauge, pump-action shotgun from the back seat of his black-and-white, and tote it along. The short-range, smoothbore weapon was not intended for any hoodlums who might be prowling about; his Colt .45 revolver would take care of any human intruders. No, the shotgun would give him the extra punch necessary to bring down the bloodthirsty Khan on the outside chance he was playing opossum somewhere, waiting for some unsuspecting soul to breach his canine sanctuary.

Deputy Sheriff Kingsley made a 360-degree scan of his surroundings and cautiously advanced toward his objective, stopping several feet shy of the main entrance.

"Well," he said aloud, "that gate is secure. No doubt about that."

The officer surveyed the yard once again for any signs of life. It was growing darker now. Kingsley thought about returning to his car to retrieve his oversized, professional-grade flashlight but decided against it.

"Hey Khan, are you in there?" he said, coaxing the dog to show himself.

Khan was either incapacitated or just wasn't buying the officer's friendly gesture, as the pooch was nowhere to be seen. Not totally convinced of the dog's intentions, Kingsley puckered his lips together and warbled out his best whistle.

"Here boy, here boy," the man called out. But there was no sign of the four-legged, canine guard anywhere. "Come on, Khan. Where the hell are you?"

Against his better judgment, Kingsley ambled right up to fence until he was a few inches away, and looked straight up. After a brief moment of reflection, he finally concluded he basically had two options facing him there. One: scale the twelve-foot fence, maneuver through the three strands of barbed wire at the top, then lower himself to the ground on the far side to have a look around; or two: return to his patrol car, drive back into town, give Earl Scrap a call on the telephone, and invite him to meet out at the salvage yard to figure out exactly what was going on. The overweight officer glanced down at his seemingly pregnant, donut and beer-infused gut, and immediately rejected option one. As it turned out, option two wasn't going to work out quite the way he planned either.

The deputy sheriff was about to retreat back to his cruiser and set out to contact Earl when an eerie clamor, originating from somewhere deep within the compound, seized his immediate attention. It sounded like a macabre choir of voices chanting some sort of unintelligible, ancient verse. Kingsley turned and bent an ear to garner a greater appreciation of the surreal symphony he was sensing from afar. Yes, he was sure of it now—a number of tiny voices singing a tune of some anomalous familiarity. Suddenly, an odd sound joined the angelic chorale, something similar to a combustible, gasoline engine. It sounded as though it was struggling to find some spark of life, but its electric starter just couldn't find the extra bit of energy necessary to turn the motor completely over. The lawman squinted his eyes to get a better look into the ever-darkening shadows. It was the last thing he would ever do in this world.

Some fifty yards away, a large, burned-out vehicle abruptly roared to life, burst into bright auburn and canary-yellow flames, rocketed across the junkyard, and blasted through the heavy-duty wire gate like a hot knife through a stick of Blue Bonnet margarine. Deputy Sheriff Mark Kingsley never knew what hit him. As the fiery Jefferson County school bus headed down Route 59, and far into the darkness beyond, the six tiny voices on board the bus continued their little ditty.

"One hundred bottles of beer on the wall, one hundred bottles of beer; take one down and pass it around, ninety-nine bottles of beer on the wall!"

Back inside the scrap yard, the only living creature to witness the whole, sordid event slowly emerged from his hiding place beneath an old, rusted-out, junkyard jalopy. He stood erect on all fours, quivering to beat the band. Khan had never been afraid of anything in his entire life. But as he lay back down in the unsettled dust of the oil-stained yard—cowering uncontrollably beneath the glow of a massive full moon—he would never again be the same dog that he was before this night's extraordinarily peculiar events.

Chapter 12

1 + 2 + 3 + 4 = 0 ?

The news about what happened at Earl Scrap's Scrap Yard spread around Jefferson County, ironically enough, like wildfire. County Sheriff Matt Kingsley, Deputy Sheriff Mark Kingsley's older brother, was not quite sure how to proceed with the investigation. Obviously this was no accident, but how could he justify pursuing the peculiar affair as a criminal matter? He had no evidence, no motive, no suspects, no leads, no witnesses, and Khan the junkyard dog would not be testifying to anything in a court of law anytime soon! No, Sheriff Matt Kingsley had absolutely nothing to go on—nothing at all.

What the lawman did have was this:

1) A recently deceased brother: cause of death, complete incineration by unknown means.

2) A heavily damaged, chain-link security gate bearing signs of metal meltdown: heat source, unknown.

3) An unaccounted-for county school bus—once big and yellow—recently crumpled and torched to a crisp: true cause of destruction, known only to the Kingsleys and Skip Summers.

4) A frightened junkyard dog, sorely in need of a canine sedative.

Matt removed the ten-gallon Stetson from his balding, Neanderthal skull and scratched his head. He was trying to reconstruct some kind of picture out of this 500-piece jigsaw puzzle; regrettably for the officer, 496 of the pieces needed to solve the riddle were missing. The county sheriff placed his hat back on his bean and silently added the evidence together in his head one more time, like a six-year-old struggling through first-grade math. No matter how many times he calculated and recalculated the problem, the result remained precisely the same: *1* + *2* + *3* + *4* = *0—nothing, nil, naught, squat, zilch, zip, zero!*

"So, what do you think?" the county coroner on the scene asked his older brother.

"I'm telling you, Luke, I've never seen anything like this before," Matt responded. "I just can't figure out why Mark didn't check in to let somebody know something might be going on out here."

"You think it might have been a burglary, Matt?"

"Why would anyone want to steal an old, burned-out school bus, Luke?"

"And that's all that's missing?"

"As far as Earl and I can tell, that's it," Matt answered.

"Well, where's that nasty old dog of Earl's?" Luke quizzed his brother. "You'd figure that a dog with Kahn's reputation would've at least got a mouthful of ass out of anybody snooping around here tonight."

"Earl found him over there hiding under an old Buick," Matt explained. "Says he can't get the damn dog to come out of there. Acts like he's in shock or some such nonsense."

"That doesn't sound like any man-eating dog to me," Luke scowled.

"Any ideas about what happened to Mark, Mister County Coroner?" the sheriff asked his younger sibling.

"Hell, no!" Luke blasted back at his brother like it was obviously a stupid question to be asking at this juncture in the investigation. "He's burned to a crisp, that's for sure. We're lucky we found his police badge nearly intact. At least that makes it a positive ID."

"So how are we supposed to track down the bastards responsible for this monstrosity without a single clue of what happened here, Luke?"

"Know anybody in the county that owns a flamethrower, Matt?"

Sheriff Kingsley was not thrilled by the comment his little brother uttered with a hint of sarcasm in his voice; but truth be told, grasping at straws was the only thing the two Kingsley boys had at the present.

Chapter 13
Twelve Names

The ebony sky was perfectly clear as a billion stars twinkled down divinely from the heavens above. The glorious, cream-colored moon—now nearly through its 28-day lunar cycle—was about to peak into full blossom once again. It was the third full moon since the bus accident back in early July, and it beamed down its soft, bewitching light, cloaking the evening landscape with countless shades of darkened shadows. It was now September 5, and the man in the moon did not look quite as sad as he had in August.

Quentin Jones, the retired school janitor and *pro bono* landscaper of the Eighth Acre memorial site, had not returned to the resting place of the eighteen young boys since his cryptic encounter some weeks ago. Why he decided to return on this ungodly night was beyond human comprehension. Nevertheless, he felt compelled to make the midnight excursion to the secluded burial ground—as an unsuspecting lemming rushes headlong toward the sea where certain annihilation awaits—without ever knowing why. Admittedly, Quentin was frightened half out of his wits the day he discovered the extraordinarily altered granite stone, but in hindsight he decided he might have been mistaken about the whole affair after all. Maybe there was a logical explanation for what he thought he saw—or didn't see—upon the mirror-polished memorial on that most peculiar morn back in early August.

As Quentin warily approached the simple, wooden archway that opened into the heart of the Eighth Acre, his flashlight wavered in his unsteady hand. The late-summer evening air lay perfectly still, and not a single cloud was visible in the moonlit sky above. Forging ahead almost against his will, the obsessed caretaker crossed the imperceptible boundary separating the real world from the bizarre realm of evil now tainting the supposed-hallow ground of the austere cemetery. Step by cautious step, Quentin moved forward. A shroud of heavy fog suddenly rolled in and descended upon his head. No flashlight ever made could possibly penetrate the thick blanket of white that now lay all around him, so he let the lamp slip from his hand and continued his voyage onward as though snared in some hypnotic trance. But Quentin knew this place like the back of his own hand, and did not require any man-made devices to light his way to journey's end. After forty unconscious paces in the blinding, midnight mist, Quentin instinctively came to a sudden halt.

Looking down through the spinning haze, he found himself standing directly in front of the memorial stone. Slowly stooping down on bended knee, Quentin brushed away the swirling vapor clinging to its base like the steamy condensation adhering to a bathroom mirror. After several moments of eying the unpretentious text engraved upon the granite stone, he rose with a trace of quiet satisfaction etched upon his face and hastily retraced his steps out of the sweltering graveyard. His speed was not seeded in the strangeness of the night, or dread of wicked spirits skulking about. On the contrary, Quentin found consolation with the fact that his eyes had indeed deceived him those several weeks before. He was now absolutely convinced he was mistaken about seeing the names of six boys on the monument gone missing. No, there was no doubt in his mind now; he was elated that he had not revealed what he *thought* he saw that day to any other living soul, lest they brand him a lunatic. Yes, he was now positive on that account. Had he confided to anyone about what he *thought* he saw on that morning after the full moon in August, it wouldn't have been long before everyone in Jefferson County was gossiping about that crazy, old Negro, Quentin Jones! Yes, the good citizens of Jefferson County would have certainly thought him insane. But on this night, Quentin learned the real truth of the whole matter. Six names were *not* missing from the memorial stone in the center of the cemetery known as the Eighth Acre after all. On this unholy night, Quentin had clearly, and without any reservation whatsoever, counted *twelve* names absent from the slab, not *six*.

Chapter 14
Five Minutes Hence

Just minutes before Quentin Jones ventured into the Eighth Acre in search of rational answers for events now some-weeks past, the blinding fog in which the caretaker ultimately found himself immersed had descended quietly from the heavens above. It consumed the small memorial park in total secrecy. The events about to transpire were not for any mortal souls to witness.

Once veiled in a camouflage of white, the transformation began in earnest. The towering, dark obelisk of polished stone at the center of the burial plot began swaying to and fro like a pendulum on a grandfather clock, and the barren soil beneath its bulk began bubbling to the surface like lava from a wakening volcano. The supernatural effect soon spread to a small area where six tiny caskets lay buried. The ground gradually swelled at that particular place until its girth could no longer be contained. The pregnant, earthen balloon burst open wide, its contents spewing forth like a hog's underbelly being splayed by a butcher's blade. What emerged from the appalling cocoon was a host of tiny, black-winged creatures resembling the dreaded locusts of Old Testament lore. The terrible minions poured from the soil, sliced though the midnight mist, and rose ever higher into the ebony sky. The dark swarm whirled and twirled, churning this way and that, until finally the shadowy fragments concluded their macabre dance in midair directly above the Eighth Acre. The cryptic spectacle quickly coalesced into a solitary figure, and then abruptly split into six surreal shapes—each one a mirror image of the others. The crude illusions resembled the black paper silhouettes police departments use for target practice: a pattern using a rectangular torso with a blocked head added at the top. The apparitions hovered in the moonlit sky for an instant, and then flashed out of sight, disappearing as quickly as they had appeared.

Five minutes hence, Quentin stood at the entrance to the Eighth Acre, seriously contemplating whether or not to violate the dense, foggy domain lying before him on that September night.

Chapter 15
Adieu, Matt & Luke Kingsley

It was exactly four-weeks' time since the first six names disappeared from the black stone at the Eighth Acre. Six more vanished as Matt, Luke, and Big John—the three surviving Kingsley brothers—gathered in their usual men-only hangout for their monthly get-together. The men were totally oblivious to the mysterious happenings out at the Little-Leaguers' cemetery.

The county lockup was a modest, brick structure that housed a small office and two holding cells in the back. No one in Jefferson County could recall the last time the jail ever held a legitimate prisoner within its walls. On occasion, the slammer did play host to a vagrant or two—usually the town drunks who were completely harmless, but nonetheless needed temporary, overnight accommodations. More often than not, the jailhouse simply served as a gathering place for the Kingsleys' once-a-month poker night. Tonight was one of those nights; except this time, one of the Kingsley boys was missing. Mark, the target of an unsolved and most peculiar crime, was lying in his grave. If he was playing cards now, he was surely in the company of the devil himself.

Big John chomped on his two-bit cigar and eyed his hand. He reached down and tossed a couple of blue, plastic chips toward the center of the green felt-covered table. "Raise you ten," he bellowed between his nicotine-stained teeth.

Luke, the youngest of the brothers and part-time county coroner, frowned and slammed his cards down in disgust. "I quit," he declared to the others sitting around the table.

"What do you mean, you quit?" Big John demanded.

"I just don't feel like playing tonight," Luke answered. "It just doesn't seem right without Mark here."

Matt downed the last of his beer and crushed the can against his forehead. "If we ever catch the bastard who did that to Mark, I swear he'll never make it to trial alive!" he bawled.

"Just who do you think you're ever going to catch?" Big John challenged. "It's been a month now, and you haven't got a damn clue about what happened!"

"Did you ever get a report back from that fancy medical examiner over in Kansas City?" Matt asked his brother Luke.

"He told me he'd never seen anything like it since his time in the Marines out in the Pacific."

"What's that supposed to mean?" Big John wanted to know.

"He told me he saw bodies of dead Japs when he served in World War II that were flushed out of their mountain caves on those islands over there. When they refused to surrender, the Marines fired them up with jellied gasoline from a flamethrower," Luke answered. "Torched them up like toasted marshmallows."

"Jesus, what a way to go," Matt sobbed openly. He already had too many beers, and had always been the sensitive sibling of the Kingsley bunch growing up. His other brothers always teased him about it. The family could not believe it when Matt announced his chosen profession would be law enforcement. They thought him too soft a touch for such a sobering occupation.

"Look," Big John declared. "If you two darlings are just going to sit here all night and cry in your beer, I'm going home!"

"Suit yourself, John," Luke countered. "You never did care much about anybody or anything did you?"

"Screw you, Luke," Big John replied as he rose from the card table. "Mark's dead, and that's that. If you two had any brains between your ears, you'd figure out who in the hell's responsible for his murder, and put a bullet in their head."

He snatched his hat and jacket off the coat rack by the door and stormed out of the jailhouse, leaving his younger brothers pining away inside. As Big John pulled out of the parking lot and headed toward home on Route 59, he noticed the moon riding high in the night sky. *Looks like it's full tonight,* he thought to himself as he sped off down the lonely road without another vehicle in sight.

The melancholy mood back inside the county jail was about to take a turn for the worst as the remaining Kingsley brothers were startled by an unsettling noise coming from the rear of the building.

"What was that?" Luke cried out.

Matt instinctively reached for his sidearm, and shrugged his shoulders in silence.

"You got anybody locked up back there?" Luke asked his older brother.

"Not that I know of, unless old man Potter snuck in here for a snooze while I was out," Matt said.

Before the county sheriff could investigate the matter, a horrendous racket erupted from the back. Luke bolted out of his chair and scrambled to his brother's side, and a metallic sound resembling multiple tin cups raking against the iron bars of a jail cell continued unabated. The loathsome noise generated a hellacious, earsplitting clamor, and sent the Kingsley boys' hearts racing to beat the band.

"Are you sure there's nobody back there?" a wide-eyed Luke nervously asked.

"There's only one way to find out," Matt whispered to his jumpy sibling.

The lawman readied his service revolver in his right hand, a flashlight in his left, and nodded for Luke to turn the door handle leading to the holding area. As Luke did so, the uproar suddenly stopped.

"Sixty bottles of beer on the wall, sixty bottles of beer; take one down and pass it around, fifty-nine bottles of beer on the wall."

Luke leaned over his brother's shoulder. "That sounds like a bunch of kids in there, Matt."

"We'll just see about that," the sheriff stated brusquely.

The door flung open, and Matt burst inside fully expecting to see anything other than what he actually saw standing before him now—absolutely nothing! He pointed his flashlight beam one way, then the other, and back again; there was nothing there except for two, very vacant holding cells.

"What is it?" Luke asked from behind, choosing not to cross the open threshold until his brother gave the okay.

"There's no one in here, Luke," Matt replied while flipping on the light switch.

"But I heard..."

"I know what you heard, little brother. I heard it too."

"But..."

"Have a look for yourself, Luke," Matt invited the skeptic.

Luke guardedly entered the back room from the outer office and discovered exactly what Matt had described—nothing out of the ordinary.

"But I know I heard voices back here, Matt."

"I know, Luke. I heard them too," the officer confirmed.

"It was like kids singing some kind of song, you know?"

"Yeah, I know, Luke. Maybe we just had a little bit too much to drink tonight."

Suddenly, all the lights in the county jail went dark. Matt toggled the electrical switch on the wall several times to no avail. He whipped his heavy-duty, police-grade flashlight back out of his utility belt and slid the switch forward. Nothing happened. No matter how many times he thrust the control back and forth, the lamp refused to light.

"Damn it," he cursed, banging the device against the wall.

Now the only illumination shining through the jailhouse gloom came from an eerie show of moonlight beaming past the small, barred windows in the pair of empty cells.

"Fifty-nine bottles of beer on the wall, fifty-nine bottles of beer; take one down and pass it around, fifty-eight bottles of beer on the wall."

"Jesus, Matt," Luke nudged his brother. "There it is again!"

"It's coming from back there," Matt said, pointing toward the cells. "Somewhere outside the building. Come on, let's have a look."

Cautiously, the two men moved forward in unison: one entering the right-hand cell, and one taking the left. They slowly inched toward the windows and had a peek outside.

"See anything, Luke?"

"Nah. I can't see a darn thing out there from here."

"Maybe we should go out around back and have a look-see," Matt suggested.

The two brothers started to turn, but never got the chance to retreat. Out of the corners of their eyes, Matt and Luke caught a quick glimpse of their impending doom, They didn't even have a chance to scream.

The rocketing fireball smashed through the brick structure like a frenzied kid with a Louisville Slugger baseball bat blasting a piñata into oblivion. The massive impact left a ten-foot-wide path of utter destruction through the center of the county sheriff's office. The flaming school bus successfully concluded its lethal intentions, fishtailed onto the highway, and blazed down Route 59. All the while, the chilling celebration of a job well done reverberated from somewhere within the smoking wreckage.

"Fifty-eight bottles of beer on the wall, fifty-eight bottles of beer; take one down and pass it around, fifty-seven bottles of beer on the wall."

Chapter 16
Rotten Eggs

When local authorities residing within the boundaries of the Sunflower State are unable to properly conduct a criminal or accident investigation—for whatever the reason—the responsibility of jurisdiction falls squarely on the shoulders of the Kansas Highway Patrol. With the only two law-enforcement officers of Jefferson County now deceased, as well as the county coroner, four highway patrol units responded to the call. Their cars sat idling with their cherry lights flashing near the scorched parking lot directly in front of what little was left of the county sheriff's office. It looked as though a low-grade atomic weapon had detonated directly on target.

As a dozen officers from the highway patrol carefully combed through the still-smoldering ruins searching for clues, Big John Kingsley arrived on the scene of catastrophic carnage. He was not a happy camper as he sought out the lead investigator on the case. John wanted answers, and he wanted them now!

"I'm sorry for your loss, Mr. Kingsley," the officer in charge expressed his condolences. "We are just in the preliminary stages of our investigation. We don't have a lot to go on."

"You must have *some* idea of what happened here last night," Big John insisted.

"Well sir, to be honest with you, if I had to make an educated guess at this point, I'd say from the looks of the damage scattered about, this was probably a gas explosion."

"A gas explosion? Are you serious?" Big John howled.

"I can't be 100-percent certain of course, until the investigation is completed, but that's what it appears to be at this juncture, sir."

"And just how do you explain those?" the elder Kingsley asked, and pointed to a set of broad, black tire tracks. They lead out of the parking lot and down the adjacent highway for some distance before magically disappearing from sight.

"Well, my forensic guy thinks they might be from a large van or another vehicle of a similar type," the officer said. "But he can't be positive just yet, and there's no telling how long those tread marks might have been there."

"I can tell you one thing, detective," Big John assured the patrolman. "Those tracks were not there yesterday!"

"All right, sir," the investigator politely acknowledged. "As I understand it, you were here with your brothers until sometime after midnight. Is there anything out of the ordinary you can recall about last night?"

"What do you mean?" John replied.

"Did you smell anything unusual before you left the premises?"

"Like what?"

"Maybe like an odor of rotten eggs?" the investigator asked.

Big John knew the investigator was barking up the wrong tree, and wasn't hesitant to say so. "This was *not* a propane-gas leak!" Big John stated emphatically.

"Do you have any other ideas?" the officer pressed.

Big John wanted to tell the detective what was really on his mind. He wanted to tell him those black marks on the pavement were made by a burnt-out school bus ferrying little kids around Jefferson County in the dead of night searching for any Kingsleys they could find. He wanted to tell the man about the supernatural forces at work here. He wanted to tell the Kansas Highway Patrolman the whole truth about what was really going on, but the saner part of his brain told him to shut the hell up and bite his tongue. Who would ever believe a busload of Little Leaguers were roaming about the countryside in search of those responsible for their dreadful demise—and the reprehensible cover-up they wanted to avenge?

"I can't say for sure," Big John declared with a case of nerves making his voice quiver. "But I know for a fact, my two brothers did not die from any propane blast."

Chapter 17
The First Full Moon of October

It was early October in the Sunflower State, and the weather was gradually turning cooler. The foliage on the deciduous trees populating the gently-rolling hills of Jefferson County were beautifully dressed in dazzling hues of browns, reds, yellows, and orange. The Jefferson County High School Hawks football team was undefeated in their first four outings of the 1960 campaign, and all the talk of the town as they prepared for their upcoming Friday-night pigskin showdown with the MacArthur Generals. These archrivals from neighboring Leavenworth County were also undefeated thus far.

Big John seemed to be the only one in the county who did not give a rat's behind about the goings-on of the local gridiron teams. He was too preoccupied with matters more serious in nature: the strange deaths of his three younger brothers, Matthew, Mark, and Luke. Big John was bound and determined to get to the bottom of the whole affair, and he was absolutely certain that the pivotal key in the murderous mystery lay in a patchwork of barren ground now known as the Eighth Acre. He couldn't be absolutely certain about his intuition, but it gnawed at his gut like a bowl of red-hot chili peppers, and there was only one way to put it all to an end.

The Earth's only natural satellite in the evening sky was full once again—the fourth full moon since the dreadful accident back in July that claimed the lives of so many young innocents. There would be two full moons in this month, the first occurring on October 3, and the second falling on the evening of October 31, Halloween night. Traditionally, the second full moon would be called a blue moon.

Big John found himself at the doorstep of the Eighth Acre with the first full moon of October hanging above him in the midnight Kansas sky. The image of the enchanting man in the moon was clearly visible as the brilliant glow of the white orb reflected off the mirror finish of the black obelisk standing tall in the center of the graveyard. There was no need for a flashlight on a well-lit night such as this, but he had one in hand in any case. Although the big man convinced himself he was not afraid of ghosts and goblins, he had decided to slap on his leather gun belt and tuck his Smith & Wesson .357 Magnum pistol safely into its holster—just in case.

Big John stood at the threshold of the hallowed ground. He surveyed the area one final time before crossing beneath the simple archway that identified the only entrance into the cemetery. As this was his first visit to the memorial site, he thought it odd to find the place so thoroughly desolate—no trees, no grass, no shrubs, no flowers—absolutely no sign of floral life anywhere within the confines of the burial ground. The place was just a strip of miserable, isolated desert with a piece of pointed stone standing smack-dab in the middle of it all. *No wonder no one ever comes out here to visit,* Big John thought to himself as he headed toward the monument. *This is really depressing!*

Depressing or not, John continued his short journey to the base of the slab that represented the eighteen youngsters interred within. Each body was tucked away in its tiny, egg-white tomb somewhere beneath the unmarked, sterile ground. John bent down and inched closer to the black stone towering before him to get a closer look at the inscription etched upon its surface.

"Gone Too Soon," it read, followed by the names of the eighteen boys buried at the Eighth Acre. Only John noticed there were not eighteen names on that stone as there should be—not even close. No, John only counted six names. How curious. John switched on his flashlight and ran the beam up and down the face of the polished rock, thinking perhaps he had simply missed the other twelve names somewhere in the shadows of the night. No, there were indeed only six names on the monument! Where were the other twelve?

What happened next was beyond John's grasp of reality. The dusty ground beneath his feet began quaking so violently, his 250-pound frame bounced uncontrollably up and down like a circus acrobat on a giant trampoline. As John struggled to regain his balance, the petrified man reached out to steady himself on the granite obelisk. It was all for naught. John was being propelled higher and higher into the night sky by a supernatural force he could not began to comprehend. Suddenly a thick, black cloud of ash gushed from the earth like an oilrig that just struck black gold. The wispy stream lifted the terrified trespasser on a torrid trajectory high into the atmosphere, leaving a trail of smoke in its wake like a Cape Canaveral rocket blasting off from its pad.

John would have screamed bloody murder if he had the time, but he did not. As John's dark silhouette streaked across the shimmering moon, he lit up like a Roman candle for a brief, sparkling moment, and then disappeared in the blinding flash of a colossal fireball. Anyone looking skyward at that very instant may have simply thought it a once-in-a-lifetime, shooting-star experience; for John Kingsley, it was the kiss of death, and his banishment from any earthly existence. Sometime later, the good citizens of Jefferson County would search for his remains, but not a trace of Big John Kingsley would ever be found.

Its work now done, the black cloud of ash miraculously transformed into six charred torsos. The figures joined their twelve companions on the burnt-out yellow school bus that lay idling in a patch of nearby woods adjacent to the Eighth Acre. The decimated vehicle ground into gear, emerged from its hiding place, and scorched down Highway 59. A choir of cheerful voices rose from within.

"Twenty-one bottles of beer on the wall, twenty-one bottles of beer; take one down and pass it around, twenty bottles on beer of the wall."

Chapter 18
A Key to the Plan

George "Skip" Summers was not the brightest bulb in the chandelier, but it didn't take Dick Tracy to figure out something bizarre was going down in Jefferson County. With the Kingsley boys out of the picture, Skip knew he was now the star attraction of some insane, Jefferson County, three-ring circus. Someone or *something* was wreaking havoc on the conspirators of the school-bus fiasco, and now four of the five people responsible for the injustice were either recently missing or deceased!

"Ladies and gentlemen, boys and girls, children of all ages, please direct your attention high overhead as that amazing daredevil himself, Skip Summers, performs a death-defying feat never before attempted by any living man. He's traversing forty, continuous feet of high wire on a death-defying trek across the Big Top, without the benefit of a safety net below, or balancing aids of any kind! Maestro, a drum roll, if you please!"

Skip was not taking one single step out on that tightrope! He wanted out of the spotlight, and he wanted out now. He wanted out of town, he wanted out of the county, and he wanted out of the state. Hell, he wanted out of the country if possible! Maybe an early retirement to some Caribbean island with crystal-clear waters and warm, ocean breezes—and a cute, local girl to keep his coconuts content. Yeah, that's the ticket! Skip was well aware that his fat, curse-of-a-wife would be coming into a heap of money with Big Daddy's inheritance, but he also knew what he would have to do to stake a claim on that cash. There was no way in hell he was going to snuggle up to titanic Gertie's revolting tonnage to make that deal a reality. Skip could stoop as low as you could go with the best of them, but not that low! Besides, no one knew for sure if Big John was dead or alive. He disappeared into thin air without a trace, and that would amount to a mountain of red tape before his estate was finally settled. The lawyers would certainly rake in a load of cash on that lengthy litigation. All Skip needed was a little money: just enough dough to get him down to that tropical paradise and into a life of anonymity. That kind of thinking necessitated some sort of a plan. Incredibly enough,

Skip truly believed he had a viable plan ever since he accidentally discovered a strange-looking key.

It was now October 31—Hallow's Eve—and Skip cruised down Highway 59 in his custom El Dorado. As usual he was drunk as a skunk, and exceeding the speed limit by twenty-five miles an hour. He had a legitimate reason for his celebratory mood: his plan had actually succeeded.

A little while back, Skip arrived home from work early: not to enjoy some quality time with his lovely spouse, but simply because he left his wallet there and didn't have so much as a dime for happy hour at the local speakeasy. To his dismay, when he did recover his billfold from his bedroom, there wasn't any cash in it anyway. That meant he had to go to the old battle-ax and cajole her into parting with a bit of cash. That was never an easy task. Gertie Summers was the keeper of the purse strings in the household, and the former Miss Gertrude Kingsley was especially stingy about giving away the personal monthly allowance from her daddy, Big John. But Gertie wasn't home, and Skip figured she must be out shopping somewhere. At first he was furious at the prospect of waiting for her return; but on second thought, Skip decided it would be a perfect opportunity to rummage through his wife's personal effects while she was out of the house.

Skip found his wife's sleeping quarters in perfect order, unlike his messy bedroom just down the hall. Skip began his search with all the drawers in her two matching nightstands without success. He moved on to her obstinate, dark-oak-finished bureau across the room—still no luck. The bedroom closet seemed to be the next logical place for his wife to stash a little extra cash. Regrettably, Skip didn't find anything of value in that cubbyhole, even after thoroughly examining eight, oversize handbags and shaking down thirteen pairs of women's shoes. Skip was left empty-handed and wondering exactly how a 350-pound beast managed to fit her beefy foot into a size 5 shoe! Before he exited the cloakroom, Skip carefully rearranged everything back to its proper place so as not to arouse any suspicion from his hefty wife. After shuffling through the bed linens and turning the pillowcases inside out, he tidied up his clutter, briefly looked under the bed, then turned his attention toward his last hope for uncovering some tiny treasure to use for drinking money: the vanity table.

Skip eyed the numerous assortments of cosmetics adorning the small, mirrored table, and questioned why Mrs. Summers even bothered trying to make herself attractive. All the makeup in the universe couldn't begin to make his triple-chinned wife any more desirable. "You can put lipstick and rouge on a pig," Skip used to tease her, "but underneath all the glitter, it's still just a pig!" Skip shuffled around every bottle, case, and container lying before him on the faux-marble tabletop, but there wasn't a single dead president hiding anywhere. He was about to turn away when he accidentally knocked his wife's pink princess phone onto the floor, dislodging the receiver from the stand, and activating the dial tone. He cursed out loud at his clumsiness, then bent down to pick up the contraption. That's when Skip noticed something shiny taped to the undersurface of the base. Skip peeled the object off the phone. He scratched away the tape and discovered a silver-colored key. It was an odd-shaped key: one that Skip did not readily recognize. Why was there some need to conceal it?

Skip repeatedly tossed the key in the air as he made his way back to the kitchen, racking his brain all the way, trying to remember where he had seen a key like this before. Try as he might, he could not solve the riddle. Skip glanced at the wall clock in the living room, looked at the Rolex on his wrist, and confirmed the time. With his disagreeable spouse probably due home at any moment, Skip decided to head back into town. Perhaps the proprietor of the local Oskaloosa bar and grill—cleverly disguised as a private club to circumvent Kansas-state liquor laws—would take his expensive timepiece as temporary collateral for a few bottles of his finest grain alcohol.

Chapter 19
The Key is the Key

It turned out the barkeep didn't need any collateral for Skip's drinks. He felt sorry for his steady customer, having lost a father-in-law and three uncles-in-law over the past several months under incredible circumstances. "I'll just put it on your tab, Skip," the bartender said as he poured the liquid refreshment into his patron's shot glass. "I know you're good for it," he smiled.

"Thanks, Ron. You're a stand-up guy." Skip drained his drink and nodded for a refill. "Ever seen one of these before, Ron?" he said while extracting the unusual key he obtained from his wife's bedroom from his breast pocket.

The barkeep examined the item for a moment. "Sure," he confirmed with authority.

"No kidding?" Skip said.

"Yeah, my old lady has one like that," Ron said. "She has a safety-deposit box over at the bank," he nodded. "She keeps some of her valuables over there. You know, a couple of pieces of jewelry and such."

"Are you sure, Ron?" Skip's face lit up.

"Sure, I'm sure. All you've got to do is walk across the street to the bank and check it out, Skip."

And that's exactly what Skip did. He trotted over to the Jefferson County First National Bank just five minutes before closing time. The bank officer was anxious to close up shop and get home, so he had no trouble believing Skip's story about his wife being too distraught over recent events to come into town and take care of banking business on her own. The banker simply had Skip sign the register and then escorted him to a secure area near the vault room. He used his master key to open one lock while Skip used his key to open the second lock. The kindly banker extracted the box from its storage compartment and set it down on a table. He instructed Skip to ring the buzzer when he had finished his affairs, then departed the premises to give Skip his privacy.

Skip slowly opened the safety-deposit box lid and peered inside. He could not believe his eyes at first, but there it was in all its finest mint-green glory—the answer to all his woes—cold, hard cash! Skip looked about quickly, making certain he was absolutely alone before tallying up the loot. Skip counted fifteen banded stacks of hundred-dollar bills. Then he counted them a second time, and a third time, just to be sure. Each wrapper bore a $10,000 denomination for a grand total of $150,000! Big Daddy John Kingsley had been very generous to his only daughter—very generous indeed! Skip quickly stuffed the cash beneath his shirt and slipped on his jacket, hoping to conceal his lumpy torso. There were a few trinkets in the safety-deposit box as well, but he decided to leave his loathsome wife a little something to remember him by. Skip pressed the button on the counter, and the bank official promptly appeared a few moments later. Together, they replaced the safety-deposit box in its proper place and exchanged parting pleasantries.

"Did you find everything to your satisfaction?" the banker asked politely.

Skip was beaming like a little kid in a candy shop. He wanted to tell the man precisely how pleased he was, but of course that was entirely out of the question.

"Yes," Skip smiled cordially. "Everything was quite satisfactory."

Chapter 20
No More Bottles of Beer on the Wall

That had all happened earlier in the afternoon, and Skip didn't waste any time hitting the road. He went home, packed a few things in a suitcase, and tossed it in the backseat of his El Dorado. He made one brief stop at a liquor store to purchase several bottles of spirits to keep him company on his drive to the airport in Kansas City. He had no idea about airline schedules departing from Kansas City's Mid-Continent International Airport that evening, but he didn't care. He'd hitch a ride on anything headed east. Eventually, he wanted to get to that Caribbean island he always dreamed about—better sooner than later.

So there he was, nouveau riche, tooling down Route 59 at eighty-five miles an hour, with the windows down and the radio blaring out a Marty Robbins' tune, *"Out in the west Texas town of El Paso, I fell in love with a Mexican girl..."* He was slightly intoxicated and totally out of control, weaving back and forth across the center dividing line near dusk, with $150,000 in tow and not a care in the world.

Suddenly, something up the highway caught his attention—a bright light of some sort heading his way. Skip slowed his car and studied the unidentified object bearing down on his position unabated. Closer and closer, the maniacal mirage screamed down the road threatening certain disaster.

"What in God's name..." Skip mumbled in his alcoholic stupor. It couldn't be what he thought he saw—a flaming, yellow school bus!

Skip covered his face and slammed on the brakes as the big, pricey Cadillac fishtailed out of control. He veered to the right, crashed through a recently repaired guardrail, and plummeted down a steep slope toward the bottom of the ravine. The El Dorado came to a stop on its roof, leaving its occupant dazed and bloodied within the pretzelized wreckage.

Skip moaned in agony as he wiped the warm blood away from his forehead and tried to assess the damage. His right leg and upper extremity were broken in several places for sure. He could see the bones sticking out of his flesh. His left shoulder was crushed between two pieces of twisted metal, but at least he was alive. He could smell the strong presence of alcohol, probably radiating from the liquor bottles that were shattered in the crash. At least he did not detect any gasoline vapors leaking from the Caddy's gas tank.

Amid all the carnage, Skip remained optimistic. His reasoning was impaired, and his body was numb to the reality of the situation; but thanks to the 100-proof whiskey coursing through his body, he actually believed a passing motorist would eventually notice the damaged guardrail from the highway and stop to investigate. Once discovered, his rescue would just be a matter of time. He urged himself to remain calm and hang on until then. He would make it out of this thing alive. He had to—the warm, tropical islands of the Caribbean were beckoning to him from afar.

A moment later Skip thought he heard a racket outside, like urgent footsteps rushing down the side of the ravine. At first he wasn't certain about the noise; maybe his brain was playing tricks on him. He tried to focus his bloodshot eyes through the shattered windshield, and cocked an ear to determine what the commotion was all about. But the day was growing darker as the sun began to set over the hilltop, and it was getting more difficult by the minute to see anything clearly from inside his flattened vehicle.

"Is anybody out there?" Skip cried out with all the strength he could muster. He listened, but there was no reply.

"I'm trapped in my car," he called out. "I need a doctor!"

Still there was no response to his pleas. Maybe his mind *was* playing tricks on him after all.

"Are you all right, sir?" a small, raspy voice called out.

"Is someone out there?" Skip groaned. He hoped he was not hallucinating.

"Do you need assistance, sir?" the raspy voice repeated. Only this time it sounded like two voices.

"I'm banged up pretty bad," Skip muttered.

"Do you need help, sir?" This time the voice was gaudier, and sounded like a dozen voices chanting in unison.

"What is wrong with you people?" Skip wailed. "Can't you see I need help, for God's sake?"

"Do you need medical aid, sir?" The chorus of mocking voices grew stronger as they multiplied in number.

"I'm hurt, you bunch of retards. Can't you see that?" Skip screamed at the tormentors he could not see.

"Are you injured, sir?" the monotone chorale continued.

"Please get me out of here," Skip sobbed.

"One bottle of beer on the wall, one bottle of beer; take one down and pass it around, no more bottles of beer on the wall."

"What the hell…" Skip muttered.

Eighteen tiny silhouettes descended out of thin air and surrounded the crumpled El Dorado. Skip thought he saw multiple figures of some sort resembling a head and a torso without arms or legs. But the heads lacked facial features of any kind: no ears, no eyes, no nose, no mouth, no chin—nothing. The limbless bodies seemed to hover just below their disconnected heads—or whatever they were—like they might disengage themselves at any moment and chart a separate course to destinations unknown. The blackened blobs were covered in soot and ash like chimney sweeps at the end of a long day's work.

"Need a light?" the ebony ghouls cackled in sarcastic harmony.

Before Skip could react, a small fireball shot into the backseat of the doomed Cadillac, which still reeked of distilled spirits from the splintered whiskey bottles. The petrified driver recoiled in horror as he watched the leather upholstery smolder, and then ignite. Slowly the small flame intensified, and crept its way toward the front compartment of the ill-fated automobile. Skip struggled to escape his impending death, but he was trapped, and his efforts were all in vain.

It was a protracted, painful burn. Even the alcohol streaming through his body could not dampen the excruciating agony of the blazing inferno that gradually consumed his unprotected flesh. Skip heard his skin sizzling like bacon in a frying pan as he screamed for mercy and cried out for an end to his unbearable suffering. The very last thing the condemned man felt was the excruciating pain of his eyeballs rupturing from their overheated sockets, splattering against the El Dorado's wood-grained dashboard with brutal force. He was almost unconscious when the end of his earthly life descended upon his twisted, writhing body like a curtain falling on the final act of a tragic play. The ensuing explosion was absolutely breathtaking. Two tons of fiery, molten metal rocketed upward, splashing across the cool, clear, crisp evening sky, and painting the mythical blue moon a bloody, crimson red on that thirty-first night of October.

The boys' work was now complete. There was nothing else for them to do in Jefferson County, or on the planet Earth for that matter. The man responsible for their deaths, and the four men who covered up the truth, were now dead themselves—and rightly so. As eighteen, diminutive, charred, disfigured bodies moved back toward the burned-out, yellow school bus, the scarlet moon shone down upon them all. One by one, the blackened corpses eagerly boarded the bus for their final field trip home. As each one found their seat, they magically took on their former boyhood bodies—smiling, laughing, and chattering all the while. With ball gloves and bats in hand, and Little-League caps perched upon their youthful heads, they were all ecstatic to be on their way at last.

The bus began to roll down Route 59, departed the asphalt roadway, and climbed effortlessly into the midnight sky. In the stillness of that Hallow's Eve night, not a sound could be heard except for a haunting chorus of sweet, children's voices echoing down from the heavens above.

"No more bottles of beer on the wall, no more bottles of beer; it's been lots of fun, but our work is done; now it's time we all disappear."

Chapter 21
Quentin's Garden

Quentin Jones knew there was something strange in the air this morning, the first day of November 1960. He wasn't exactly sure what might be afoot, but something was bound to be different about the Eighth Acre on this chilly day—of that, he was certain. Last night, poor Skip Summers drove his fancy El Dorado right off the road and into a ravine at precisely the same spot where the doomed school bus took its plunge some three months earlier with all those innocent kids aboard. Quentin had no doubt in his mind; Skip's accident and the Eighth Acre were surely connected in some grisly way. Quentin would have come the night before, but he could not garner the courage to make an unaccompanied journey to the spine-chilling plot under the watchful eye of that eerie, scarlet moon. No, he preferred to wait for the security of daylight.

As the memorial's self-appointed caretaker approached the archway to the Eighth Acre, he could not believe his eyes. Indeed, at first sight, he thought he might be dreaming. The tiny plot was covered with spectacular vegetation of every description! There was a two-inch-thick carpet of Kentucky bluegrass blanketing the once-inhospitable burial ground—the sort of majestic, summer grasses that beg invitation to those who would stroll through its verdure without want of footwear of any design. The wooden, split-rail fence was adorned with creeping honeysuckle, orange trumpet vines, and baby-blue wisteria. There were endless mounds of black-eyed Susans, lavender-blue asters, daylilies of every color, scarlet hollyhocks, carnations, brilliant-red coral bells, pink dragon flowers, blue salvia, fragrant lilacs of every hue, giant daisies with sunshine-yellow centers, and scores of other flora that Quentin could not begin to identify. The Eighth Acre had magically transformed into the most serene, stunning place on the Earth—and all of this magnificent, midsummer foliage on the first day of November!

There was also something extraordinary about the memorial obelisk in the center of the court. It was no longer a chilling, austere, black stone with no hint of feeling or soul. Now it appeared as white as the purest-driven snow that ever did decorate a Kansas landscape. There was radiance about the monument now, like the soft glow of a golden halo surrounding a heavenly angel's crown. With all these enchanting reformations, Quentin was no longer fearful of the Eighth Acre, nor would he ever be again.

In the years to come, Quentin would spend many comforting hours in his personal Garden of Eden—a garden that needed no tending of any sort. It remained perpetually beautiful all the year round: truly one of God's most beautiful creations. The folks in Jefferson County thought Quentin most peculiar—and quite possibly insane—when they spied him sitting in the middle of the Eighth Acre at any time of the year, day or night. He would leisurely daydream for hours on end amid the desolate cemetery plot where nothing had ever grown, nor would it ever. Of course, the ordinary folk could not see what the retired janitor could see; he alone was given a special gift of vision that enabled him to see much more than any conventional human eye might ever see.

Chapter 22
1973

Thirteen years later, in October 1973, Jefferson County experienced another true, blue moon. Quentin Jones was in his beloved cemetery that night, but he did not see a blue moon in the cool, crisp, evening sky. Instead he saw a magnificent, scarlet-red moon that warmed his heart with breathtaking delight as he slowly lay down his head and closed his weary eyes.

The next morning, a passerby discovered Quentin lying crumpled on his side, almost covered with wintry drifts from an unexpected, early-season snowfall. His once-dark skin had become as white as the fallen snowflakes that now obscured his lifeless, rigid body. The morning sun began to slowly warm the icy, autumn air, and the snow on the memorial obelisk began to melt. As the frozen flakes returned to their liquid state, it appeared as though the monument was actually shedding tears for the old man lying motionless at its base.

Having no relatives of any sort, the good folks of Jefferson County thought it appropriate to lay Quentin to rest in the place where he had spent most of his days for the last thirteen years of his pathetic life. They could not see what Quentin had seen all those marvelous years inside the small confines of the Eighth Acre. And unlike the majority of his fellow citizens residing in Jefferson County, Quentin Jones died a very happy, peaceful man.

Epilogue
1992

In 1992, DNA evidence was used to prove that the notorious, Nazi doctor, Josef Mengele, who performed "human experiments" on concentration camp inmates in Germany during World War II, was buried in Brazil under the assumed name of Wolfgang Gerhard. Thus brought an end to the search for one of the world's most sought-after war criminals in the history of all mankind.

In that same year, the surviving parents of the eighteen deceased youngsters lying in the Eighth Acre petitioned the courts for approval to have the bodies of their boys exhumed, and positively identified using the relatively new technology of DNA profiling. With the court's blessing, all eighteen of the tiny, white caskets were painstakingly recovered from their sacred burial ground, and carefully opened one by one. Strangely enough, when the insides of the satin-lined coffins were thoroughly examined for the first time in some thirty-two years, not a single shred of DNA evidence was found. Nothing was ever produced to indicate any trace of human remains had ever lain within the confines of those imagined, burial tombs.

Printed in Great Britain
by Amazon